EASY KEYBOARD BUMPER BOOK
EASY MUSIC FOR ALL KEYBOARDS
BY ROGER EVANS

CW00506494

100 GREAT TUNES
TO PLAY AND ENJOY
ALL SPECIALLY ARRANGED
FOR KEYBOARDS BY ROGER EVANS

First Published 1989
©International Music Publications Limited,
Southend Road, Woodford Green, Essex IG8 8HN, England.

Reproducing this music in any form is illegal and forbidden
by the Copyright, Designs and Patents Act 1988.

EASY KEYBOARD BUMPER BOOK
EASY MUSIC FOR ALL KEYBOARDS
BY ROGER EVANS

Easy music for all keyboards

All music specially arranged for keyboards by Roger Evans

Introduction

Welcome to the Easy Keyboard Bumper Book.

This collection of 100 tunes has been specially chosen to give you a broad variety of good-sounding music to play on your keyboard. Here you will find classic pop songs, love songs, easy rock music, motown classics, theme songs from great films, show tunes, tunes which have become jazz classics, tunes with latin and calypso rhythms — and more.

Each tune has been chosen because it sounds good on modern keyboards — and all music is specially arranged to be easy and enjoyable to play. All tunes are in easy keys and have easy chords.

This music is perfect for everyone who learned to play with the Playing Keyboards book and cassette. It is also ideal for everyone who wants to play good music easily on modern keyboard instruments.

Playing Hints

The music in this book follows the same easy style used in the *Playing Keyboards* books:

Suggested Voices and Rhythms are given at the beginning of every tune, like this:

> Organ/Flute
> Ballad/Pops or Rock (Medium)

You can choose whichever settings suit your keyboard. Here, you could choose either the Organ or Flute voice, and set a Ballad, Pops or Rock rhythm.

The suggested Tempo (speed) of the music is given in brackets like this: (Medium). Adjust the Tempo control on your keyboard to this suggested setting before you begin each tune. (If you like, set the Tempo slower than suggested until you are comfortable playing a new tune).

If your keyboard does not have any of the suggested voices or rhythms, choose voices and rhythms which suit the music you are playing.

Special Effects which you can add to the music are shown in brackets over some tunes:

(Arpeggio/Variation) — means you can add an automatic 'Arpeggio' to the backing of a tune if your keyboard has this effect; or you can use an auto chord accompaniment 'variation' which gives a 'rippling' effect.

Fingering — Finger numbers are shown in front of notes where the fingering is not obvious, and where the fingers need to move to different keys:

1 = thumb   2 = index finger   3 = middle finger   4 = ring finger   5 = little finger

Chords — You can play all of the music in this book with easy 'One Finger Chords', 'Casio Chords' or 'Single Finger Chords' — or you can use 'Fingered Chords'.

Chord symbols are shown over the music wherever a chord change is needed. Chords shown in brackets are optional, and may be left out for easy playing:

C(7) — means you can play a C7 chord, or a C chord.

(C7) — means this chord is not essential and may be left out if necessary.

All of the tunes are easier to play if the optional chords are left out. However, you will find the music usually sounds far better if *all* chords are played, so try and play them all if you can.

'Transposing' — Many keyboards have a very useful facility called a 'Transposer' which changes the pitch of the instrument. This is very helpful for music which is too high or too low for singing, and the 'Transposer' can also be used when you play along with certain other musical instruments, and for special effects.

For singing — If the music is too high for the singer, try setting the Transposer to B♭ (♭2 or -2). If the music is still too high, try setting it to G (♭5 or -5).

If the music is too low for the singer, try setting the Transposer to E♭ (#3 or +3) or F (#5 or +5).

Playing With Other Instruments — If you have friends who play B♭ instruments like the clarinet, trumpet or tenor saxophone, and you would them to play along with you, *and read your music,* set the Transposer to B♭ (♭2 or -2). For E♭ instruments set the Transposer to E♭ (#3 or +3).

(There is no need to use the Transposer when you play along with a guitar, flute, violin, recorder or most other instruments — as long as they 'tune' to your keyboard.)

You can also use the Transposer to give music a 'lift'. Try playing a tune through once. Then, without stopping, set the Transposer to C# (#1 or +1), D (#2 or +2) or higher — and play the tune again. (As with all special effects, it is best not to over-use this trick!)

Always remember to re-set the Transposer to C (0) when you have finished.

You can find more playing hints, easy-to-follow instruction and more good tunes in the *Playing Keyboards* book and songbooks, which are obtainable from your music dealer.

Wishing you many happy hours playing the music in this book.

Roger Evans

Alone

Words and Music by
BILLY STEINBERG and TOM KELLY

Trumpet/Brass or Jazz Organ/Organ 2
Rock or Ballad/Pops (Medium-Slow)
(Add Arpeggio/Variation)

© 1987 & 1989 Billy Steinberg Music & Denise Barry Music
Warner Chappell Music Ltd, London W1Y 3FA

'til now — I al-ways got by — on my

own, I nev-er real-ly cared un-til I met you.

And now it chills me to the bone.

How do I get — you a - lone?

1.

How do I get— you a - lone?

2.

lone, a - lone, ——— a -

lone?———

Instrumental* ———————

*The instrumental is optional and may be left out if you wish.

And I Love You So

Words and Music
by DON McLEAN

Violin/Strings
Ballad/Pops (Medium)

© 1971, 1972 & 1989 Mayday Music/Muziekuitgeverij Artemis BV/Intersong Music Ltd
Intersong Music Ltd, London W1Y 3FA

Arthur's Theme (Best That You Can Do)

Words and Music
by BURT BACHARACH, CAROLE BAYER SAGER,
CHRISTOPHER CROSS and PETER ALLEN

Trumpet/Brass
Ballad/Pops or Bossa Nova (Medium)

Once in your life — you'll find — her,
Ar - thur, he does — what he pleas — es.

Some-one who turns— your heart a - round, and
All of his life, — his mas - ter's toys, and

next thing you know— you're clos - in'
deep in his heart— he's just, he's

down the town.
just a boy.

Instrumental

Wake up and she's— still with — you
Liv - in' his life— one day at a time, he's

ev - en though you left her way — a - cross town. You're
show-ing him- self — a real — ly good time. He's

won - der - in' to — your - self, hey,
laugh- in' a - bout — the way they

© 1981 & 1989 WB Music Corp, New Hidden Valley Music, Begonia Melodies Inc, Unichappell Music Inc
Pop 'n' Roll Music, Woolnough Music and Irving Music Inc
All rights administered by WB Music Corp & Warner-Tamerlane Publishing Corp
Warner Chappell Music Ltd, London W1Y 3FA

what-'ve I found?
want him to be.

Instrumental —

When you get caught be-tween the moon and New York

Ci — ty.———— I know it's cra - zy,

but it's true.————

If you get caught be-tween the moon and New York

Ci —————— ty,———— the best that you can do,

the best that you can do

is fall—— in love.————

Baker Street

Words and Music
by GERRY RAFFERTY

Saxophone/Trombone or Jazz Organ
8-beat or Rock (Medium)

INTRO (Optional) Play Instrumental on next page.

Verse: Wind-ing your way down on Bak - er Street,
This city des-ert makes you feel so cold. He's got

light in your head and dead on your feet. Well, an -
so many peo-ple but he's got no soul. And it's

- oth - er cra - zy day you'll drink the night a - way and for -
tak - ing so long to find out you were wrong when you

- get a - bout ev - 'ry - thing.
thought it held ev - 'ry - thing.

Chorus: You used to think that it was so ea - sy.
An - oth - er year and then you'll be hap - py.

You used to see that it was so ea - sy, But you're try - in',
Just one more year and then you'll be hap - py, But you're cry - in',

1. you're try - in' now.
2. now.
you're cry - in'
now.

© 1976 & 1989 Gerry Rafferty
Sub-published by EMI Music Publishing Ltd, London WC2H 0EA

INSTRUMENTAL (& Intro)

Verse 2. Way down the street there's a lot in his place
He opens his door he's got that look on his face
And he asks you where you've been
You tell him who you've seen and you talk about anything.

He's got this dream about buyin' some land, he's gonna
Give up the booze and the one night stands and
Then you'll settle down with some quiet little town
And forget about everything.

Chorus 2. But you know you'll always keep movin'
You know he's never gonna stop movin'
'Cause he's rollin', he's the rollin' stone.

When you wake up it's a new mornin';
The sun is shinin', it's a new mornin'
And you're goin', you're goin' home.

Ben

Words by DON BLACK
Music by WALTER SCHARF

Flute or Violin
Ballad/Pops (Medium-Slow)

Ben, the two of us need look no more,

we both found what we were look-ing for,

with a friend to call my own, I'll nev-er be a-

-lone, and you, my friend, will see you've got a friend in

me. _____ Ben, you're al-ways run-ning

here and there, you feel you're not want-ed an-y-where

If you ev-er look be-hind and don't like what you

© 1971, 1972 & 1989 Jobete Music Co Inc,
Jobete Music (UK) Ltd, Tudor House, 35 Gresse Street, London W1P 1PN

Blueberry Hill

Words and Music by
AL LEWIS, LARRY STOCK
and **VINCENT ROSE**

Jazz Organ/Organ 2 or Trumpet
Slow Rock (Medium)

© 1940 & 1989 Chappell & Co Inc, USA
Chappell Music Ltd, London W1Y 3FA

Breaking Up Is Hard To Do

Words and Music by
NEIL SEDAKA and HOWARD GREENFIELD

Violin/Strings or Jazz Organ
Regular version: Ballad/Pops or Rock (Medium-Fast)
Slow version: Ballad/Pops

© 1962 & 1989 Screen Gems-EMI Music Inc, USA
Sub-published by Screen Gems-EMI Music Ltd, London WC2H 0EA

break-in' up is hard to do. They say that break-in'

up is hard—— to do; now I know——

I know that it's true. Don't say this is the end. In-

-stead of break-in' up I wish that we were mak-in' up a-gain.

I beg of you———— don't say good - bye;

can't we give our love an-oth-er try? Come on ba-by, let's

start a-new, Break-in' up is hard to do.

By The Time I Get To Phoenix

Words and Music by JIM WEBB

Trombone/Trumpet or Jazz Organ
Ballad/Pops (Medium-Slow)

By the time —— I get to Phoe-nix —— she'll be ris-ing, ——————————— She'll find my note I left hang-ing—— on her door. ——————————— She'll laugh when she reads the part—— that says I'm leav-ing——————— 'Cos I've left that girl—— so man-y times be-fore. ——————— By the time —— I make Al-bu-quer-que—— she'll be work-ing, ——————— She'll prob-a-bly stop at lunch—— and give me a

© 1966 & 1989 Johnny Rivers Music, all rights assigned to the EMP Co, USA
Carlin Music Corp, London W1X 2LR

Can't Help Falling In Love

Words and Music by GEORGE WEISS,
HUGH PERETTI and LUIGI CREATORE

Organ/Organ 1
Slow Rock or Ballad/Pops (Medium-Slow)
(Add Arpeggio/Variation)

© 1961 & 1989 Gladys Music Inc, USA
Carlin Music Corp, London W1X 2LR

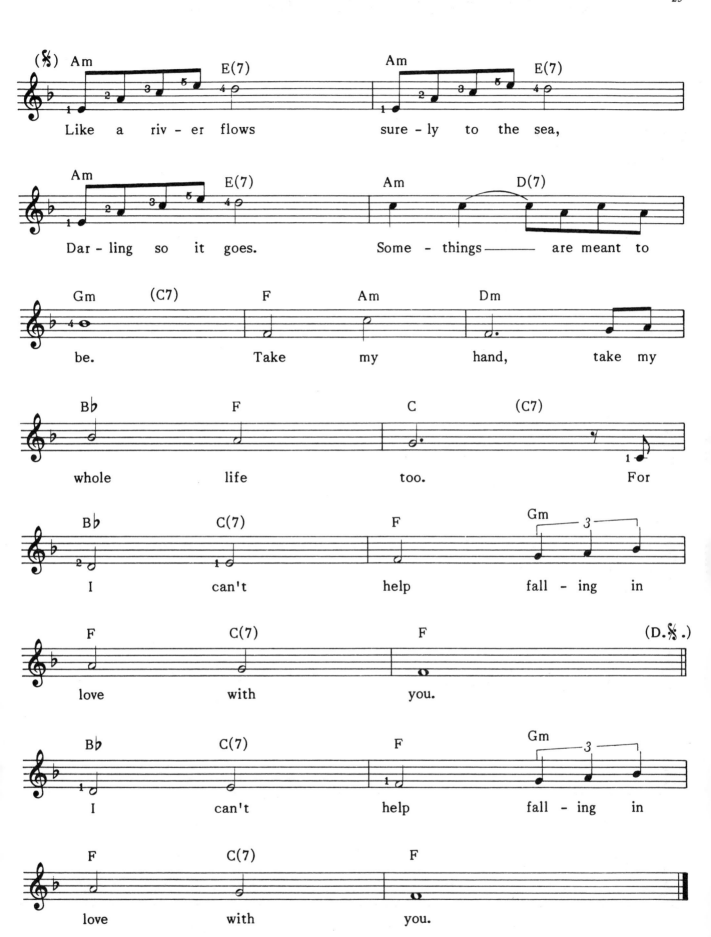

Cavatina (Theme from 'The Deerhunter')

By STANLEY MYERS

Organ or Violin/Strings
Slow Rock (Medium-Slow) or Waltz (Slow)
(Add Arpeggio/Variation)

© 1971 & 1989 Robbins Music Corp, Ltd, London WC2H 0EA

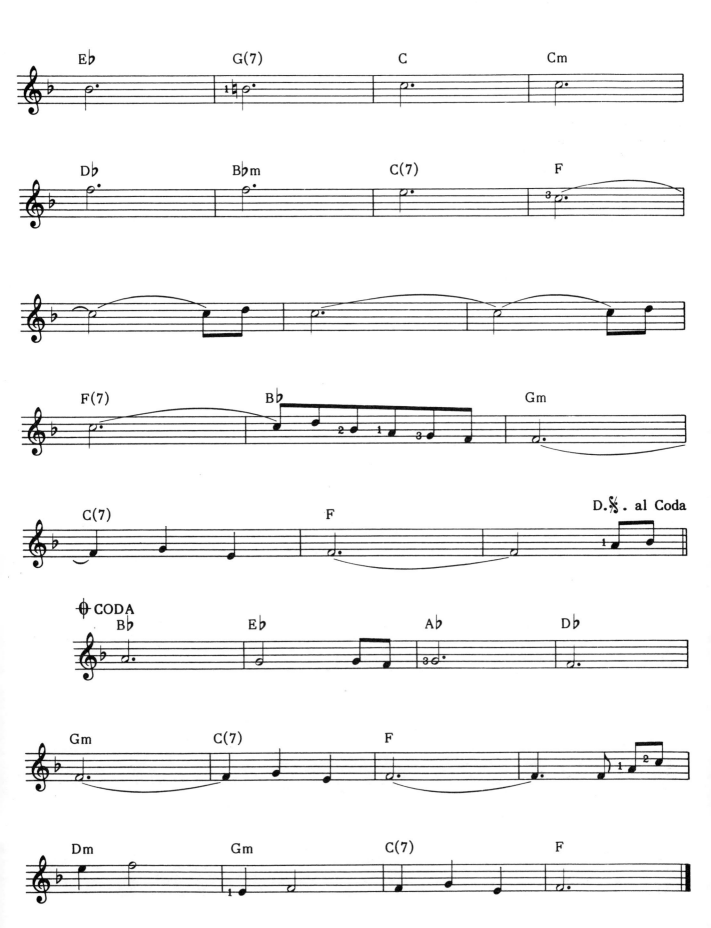

Chariots Of Fire

Composed by **VANGELIS**

Piano/Electric Piano or Guitar
Slow Rock (Medium-Slow)
(Add Stereo Chorus/Stereo Symphonic)

© 1981 & 1989 Spheric BV
Warner Chappell Music Ltd, London W1Y 3FA

The Christmas Song
(Chestnuts Roasting On An Open Fire)

Words and Music by
MEL TORME and ROBERT WELLS

Accordion or Trombone/Trumpet
Ballad/Pops (Medium-Slow)

© 1946 & 1989 Edwin H Morris & Co Inc, USA
Chappell Morris Ltd, London W1Y 3FA

Close To You (They Long To Be)

Words by HAL DAVID
Music by BURT BACHARACH

Flute, Jazz Organ or Electric Piano
Ballad/Pops or Bossa Nova (Medium)

© 1963 & 1989 US Songs Inc, USA
Carlin Music Corp, London W1X 2LR

cid - ed to cre - ate a dream come true   So they

sprink-led moon-dust in your hair—— Of   gold, and star-light in your eyes of

blue.——————   That   is

why   all the boys in   town   fol - low

you   all a - round   Just like me

they long   to be   close   to   you ———

x3   Ah ————

Close   to   you. ———

Repeat and Fade

Country Gardens

Adapted and Arranged
by ROGER EVANS

Trumpet/Brass or Flute/Clarinet
Ballad/Pops or Slow Rock (Medium)
(Add Arpeggio/Variation)

© 1989 International Music Publications, Woodford Green, Essex IG8 8HN

Cry Me A River

Words and Music
by ARTHUR HAMILTON

Flute/Clarinet or Jazz Organ
Ballad/Pops (Medium-Slow)

Now you say you're lone - ly,

You cry the long night through, Well you can

cry me a riv - er, Cry me a riv - er,

I cried a riv - er o - ver you. Now you say you're

sor - ry, For be - in' so un -

- true, Well, you can cry me a riv - er,

Cry me a riv - er I cried a riv - er o - ver

© 1953, 1955 & 1989 Chappell & Co Inc
Chappell Music Ltd, London W1Y 3FA

Dancing In The Street

Words and Music by WILLIAM STEVENSON,
MARVIN GAYE and IVY HUNTER

Trumpet/Brass or Organ
Rock (Medium - Slow)

© 1964 & 1989 Jobete Music Co Inc, USA
Jobete Music (UK) Ltd, Tudor House, 35 Gresse Street, London W1P 1PN

Dark Eyes

New Arrangement
by ROGER EVANS

Violin/Strings or Electric Guitar
Rock or March (Medium-Fast)

© 1989 International Music Publications, Woodford Green, Essex IG8 8HN

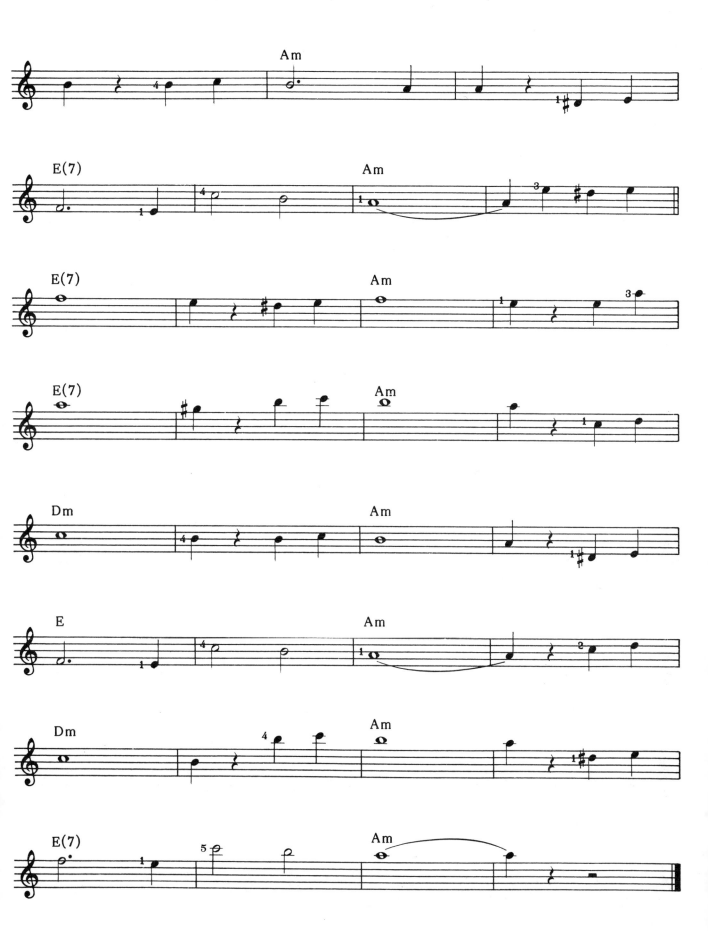

Do You Know Where You're Going To?
(Theme from 'Mahogany')

Words by GERRY GOFFIN
Music by MIKE MASSER

Organ or Violin/Strings
Ballad/Pops (Medium)
(Add Arpeggio/Variation)

© 1973 & 1989 Screen Gems-EMI Music Inc, USA and Jobete Music Co Inc, USA
Sub-published by Screen Gems-EMI Music Ltd, London WC2H 0EA

The Dock Of The Bay (Sittin' On)

Words and Music by
STEVE CROPPER and OTIS REDDING

Jazz Organ or Electric Guitar
8-beat/Rock (Medium)

© 1967 & 1989 East/Time/Redwal
Warner Chappell Music Ltd, London W1Y 3FA

Verse 3. Sittin' here resting my bones, and the loneliness won't leave me alone.
Two thousand miles I roam just to make this dock my home
Now I'm just sittin' on the dock of the bay, watchin' the tide roll away
Just sittin' on the dock of the bay. Yes, the tide. **(To Coda)**

Easy

Words and Music
by LIONEL RICHIE

Violin/Strings or Clarinet
Ballad/Pops (Slow)

© 1976 & 1989 Jobete Music Co Inc/Libren Music, USA
Jobete Music (UK) Ltd, Tudor House, 35 Gresse Street, London W1P 1PN

Easy Lover

Words by PHIL COLLINS
Music by PHILIP BAILEY,
PHIL COLLINS and NATHAN EAST

Organ/Organ 1 or Electric Guitar
Rock (Medium-Fast)

© 1984 & 1989 Phil Collins Ltd/Hit & Run (Publishing) Ltd
Pun Music Inc/Sir and Trini Music and New East Music
Warner Chappell Music Ltd, London W1Y 3FA

You'll nev-er get it.—— She will
You'll nev-er get it.—— 'Cause she'll

play a-round and leave you, leave you and de-ceive you.
say that there's no oth - er, till she finds an - oth - er.

Bet-ter for - get it. Oh, you'll re -
Bet-ter for - get it. Oh, you'll re -

- gret it.—— No you'll nev-er change her, so
- gret it.—— And don't try to change her. Just

leave her, leave her. Get out quick 'cause see-ing is be-liev-ing. It's the
leave her, leave her. You're not the only one, and see-ing is be-liev-ing.

on - ly way—— you'll ev - er know.——

1. She's an ea—— sy lov— 2. She's an ea—— sy lov—

—— er. (Instrumental) ——

Repeat and fade

El Condor Pasa

Adapted and Arranged
by ROGER EVANS

Flute
March (Medium)

© 1989 International Music Publications, Woodford Green, Essex IG8 8HN

Endless Love

Words and Music
by LIONEL RICHIE

Jazz Organ or Trumpet
Ballad/Pops (Medium-Slow)

© 1981 & 1989 PGP Music/Brockman Music/Muziekuitgeverij Artemis BV/Intersong Music Ltd
Intersong Music Ltd, London W1Y 3FA

* For short version, finish here.

The Entertainer

Music by SCOTT JOPLIN
Adapted and Arranged
by ROGER EVANS

Piano/Guitar or Clarinet/Flute
March or Country (Medium)

© 1989 International Music Publications, Woodford Green, Essex IG8 8HN

Evergreen

Words by PAUL WILLIAMS
Music by BARBRA STREISAND

Flute or Jazz Organ/ Organ 2
Bossa Nova or Ballad/Pops (Medium)

© 1976 & 1989 Artists Music Co, Emanuel Music Corp and 20th Century Music Corp
All rights administered by WB Music Corp
Warner Chappell Music Ltd, London W1Y 3FA

Everything I Own

Words and Music
by DAVID GATES

Organ/Organ 1
Reggae or Rock (Medium)

© 1972 & 1989 Screen Gems-EMI Music Inc, USA
Sub-published by Screen Gems-EMI Music Ltd, London WC2H 0EA

Everything Is Beautiful

Words and Music
by **RAY STEVENS**

Flute/Clarinet or Vibes
Ballad/Pops or Swing (Medium)

© 1970 & 1989 Ahab Music Co Inc, USA
Sub-published by EMI Music Publishing Ltd, London WC2H 0EA

he who will not see ——
col - our of his skin ——

We must not close our minds, —— we must
Don't worry about what shows from without, but the

let our thoughts be free. ——
love that lives with - in. ——

For ev - 'ry hour that pass - es by ——
We gon - na get it all to - geth - er now ——

You know the world gets a lit - tle bit old — er,
and ev - 'ry-thing gon - na work out fi —— ne,

It's time to re - a - lize that beau - ty lies in the
Just take a lit - tle time to look on the good side my friend and

eyes —————— of the be - hold —— er.
straighten it out in your mind.—

1. F

Ev - 'ry - thing is

2.*   **D. % al Fine**

Ev - 'ry - thing is

(* *If your keyboard has a 'Transposer', you could use it to change key at this point by*
setting it to +2, #2 or D.)

Every Time You Go Away

Words and Music
by DARYL HALL

Saxophone or Electric Guitar/Trumpet
Ballad/Pops (Medium-Slow)

© 1980 & 1989 Hot-Cha Music Co/Six Continents Music Publishing Inc, USA
Intersong Music Ltd, London W1Y 3FA

For Once In My Life

Words by RONALD MILLER
Music by ORLANDO MURDEN

Jazz Organ
Rock (Medium)

© 1965 & 1989 Jobete Music Co Inc, USA
© 1967 & 1989 Jobete Music (UK) Ltd, Tudor House, 35 Gresse Street, London W1P 1PN

63

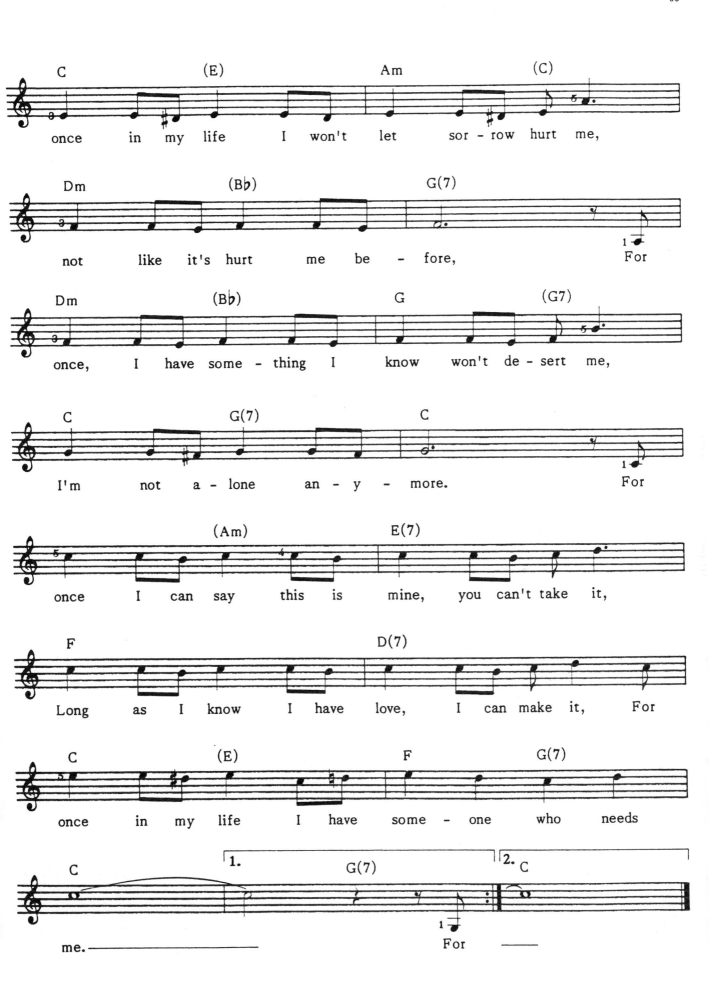

A Groovy Kind Of Love

Words and Music by
TONI WINE and CAROLE BAYER SAGER

Electric Piano/ Piano or Jazz Organ
Ballad/Pops (Medium-Slow)

When I'm feel-in' blue all I have to do is take a look at you Then I'm not so blue when you're close to me I can feel your heart beat I can hear you breath-ing in my ear. Would- n't you a- gree ba - by you and me got a groo-vy kind of love An - y-time you want to you can turn me on to an- y-thing you want to an - y time at all. When I kiss your lips, oo, I start to shiv -er, can't con-trol the quiv - er - ing in - side.— Would- n't you a-

© 1965 & 1989 Screen-Gems-Columbia Music Inc, USA
EMI Music Publishing Ltd, London WC2H 0EA

gree, ba - by you and me got a groo-vy kind of love.

When I'm feel-in' blue all I have to do is take a look at

you Then I'm not so blue. When I'm in your arms noth-ing seems to

mat - ter, my world could shat - ter I don't care.— Would - n't you a-

gree ba - by you and me got a groo-vy kind of love

We've got a groo-vy kind of love We've got a groo- vy kind of

love Oh —————————————

We've got a groo-vy kind of love. ————————

(**If your keyboard has a 'Transposer', you could use it to change key at this point
by setting it to +2, ♯2, or D.)**

Help Me Make It Through The Night

Words and Music
by KRIS KRISTOFFERSON

Electric Guitar/Electric Piano or Trumpet
Country or Rock (Medium)
(Add Arpeggio/Variation)

© 1969 & 1989 Combine Music Corp, USA
Sub-published by EMI Music Publishing Ltd, London WC2H 0EA

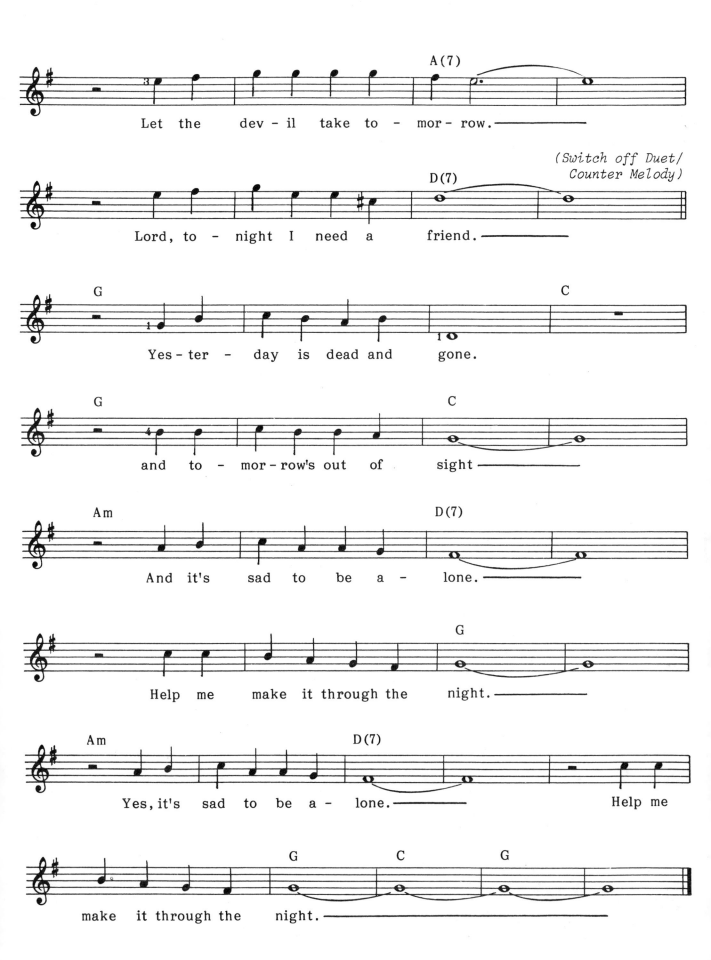

Hi Ho Silver Lining

Words and Music by
SCOTT ENGLISH and LAURENCE WEISS

Electric Guitar or Trombone/Trumpet
Rock/8-beat or Disco (Medium)

© 1967 & 1989 Helios Music Corp. B.M.I. PO Box 1182 New York NY 10101 USA

Hotel California

Words and Music by DON FELDER,
DON HENLEY and GLENN FREY

Organ or Electric Guitar
Rock/8 beat or Ballad/Pops (Medium)
(Add Arpeggio or Variation)

©1976, 1977 & 1989 Long Run Music, Fingers Music, WB Music Corp
Warner Chappell Music Limited, London W1Y 3FA

Then she lit up a can-dle, and she showed me the way.
And still those voices are calling from far a - way;

There were voices down the cor - ri - dor; — I thought I heard them say: —
wake you up in the middle of the night just to hear them say: —

CHORUS: *(Last Chorus add Duet/Counter melody)*

"Wel-come—to the Ho — tel Cal-i-for —— nia. Such a
"Wel-come—to the Ho — tel Cal-i-for —— nia. Such a

love—ly place,— (Such a love— ly place,)—Such a love— ly face.—
love—ly place,—(Such a love—ly place,)—Such a love—ly face.—

Plen-ty of room— at the Hot-el Cal - i-for —— nia. An - y
They livin' it up— at the Hot-el Cal - i-for —— nia. What a

time— of year,—(an-y time— of year,)—you can find— it here."—
nice—surprise;—(What a nice—surprise;)—bring your al — i-bis."——

*Last time: Repeat chords from the beginning
and fade out by gradually reducing the volume.*

Verse 3

Mirrors on the ceiling, the pink champagne on ice, *and she said:*
"We are all prisoners here, of our own device."
And in the master's chambers, they gathered for the feast.
They stab it with their steely knives, but they just can't kill the beast.
Last thing I remember, I was running for the door.
I had to find the passage back to the place I was before.
"Relax," said the night man, "We are programmed to receive.
You can check out any time, but you can never leave."

Chorus

House Of The Rising Sun

Adapted and Arranged
by ROGER EVANS

Organ
Slow Rock (Medium–Slow)
(Add Arpeggio/Variation)

© 1989 International Music Publications, Woodford Green, Essex IG8 8HN

I Got You Babe

Words and Music
by SONNY BONO

Trombone/Trumpet or Jazz Organ
Reggae/Rock (Medium) – UB40 Version
Slow Rock (Medium) – Sonny & Cher

*Change Key here, from F with one flat in the key signature (B♭) to G with one sharp(F♯)

© 1965 & 1989 Cotillion Music Inc, USA
Carlin Music Corp, London W1X 2LR

then they say your hair's too long, But I don't care with you I can't do wrong. Then

put your lit-tle hand in mine There ain't no hill or mountain we can't climb,

babe, I got you, babe I got you, babe.

I got you to hold my hand, I got you to un-der-stand,——

I got you to walk with me, I got you to talk with me

I got you to kiss good-night, I got you to hold me tight,——

I got you, I won't let go I got you who loves me so,

I got you, babe.

+Switch off Synchro (with your right hand).

I Guess That's Why They Call It The Blues

Words and Music by ELTON JOHN,
BERNIE TAUPIN and DAVEY JOHNSTONE

Organ
Slow Rock (Medium)

© 1983 Big Pig Music Ltd, London W1Y 3FA

I Heard It Through The Grapevine

Words and Music by
NORMAN WHITFIELD and BARRETT STRONG

Organ or Trumpet
Rock, 8-beat or Disco (Medium)

© 1966 & 1989 Jobete Music Co Inc
Jobete Music (UK) Ltd, Tudor House, 35 Gresse Street, London W1P 1PN

A
Not much — long - er would you be mine
Not much — long - er would you be mine
Em (A) (Em)
Heard it through the grape - vine
I heard it through the grape - vine
A
Oh, I'm just a - bout to lose — my
And, I'm just a - bout to lose — my
Em To Coda 1.
mind. mind. Hon-ey, hon- ey, oh yeah. 2. I know a man
2. D.S. al Coda
Ooh. —
* 3. Peo - ple say be-lieve half
CODA
x2
Hon - ey, hon - ey I know
(Fade)
that you're let - ting me go.

* **Verse 3.** (People say believe half) of what you see
Son, and none of what you hear;
But I can't help but be confused
If it's true please tell me dear,
Do you plan to let me go
For the other guy you loved before.

I Only Have Eyes For You

Words by AL DUBIN
Music by HARRY WARREN

Trumpet/Brass or Jazz Organ/Organ 2
Swing (Medium - for a jazzy feeling)
or Slow Rock (Medium-Slow)

© 1934 & 1989 Remick Music Corp, USA
Sub-published by B Feldman & Co Ltd, London WC2H 0LD

The Ice Cream Song (O Sole Mio)

Music by E. DI CAPUA
Adapted and Arranged
by ROGER EVANS

Violin/Strings
Bossa Nova (Medium)

INTRO: Backing only —————

© 1989 International Music Publications, Woodford Green, Essex IG8 8HN

If I Were A Rich Man

Words by SHELDON HARNICK
Music by JERRY BOCK

Clarinet/Flute or Violin/Strings
March (Medium)

© 1964 & 1989 Times Square Music Publications Co, USA
Carlin Music Corp, London W1X 2LR

real wooden floors be - low.
meals to her hearts' de - light.
There could be one long stair - case
I see her put - ting on airs and

just go-ing up and one ev-en longer coming down;
strutting like a peacock, Oy! What a hap-py mood she's in.
And one more lead-ing
Screaming at the

no - where just for show.
ser - vants day and night.
I'd fill my yard with chicks and
If I were rich, I'd have the

tur-keys and geese and ducks for the town to see and hear;
time that I lack, To sit in the syn - agogue and pray;
Squawk-ing just as
And may - be have a

noi - si - ly as they can
seat by the east - ern wall.
And each loud quack and cluck and
And I'd dis - cuss the ho - ly

gob - ble and honk, Will land like a trumpet on the ear;
books with the learn-ed men sev-en ho - urs ev-'ry day;
As if to say here
This would be the

1. G(7)
2. G(7) D.%. al Coda

lives a wealth-y man. —————— (sigh)
sweet-est thing of all. (sigh)

CODA

Lord, who made the li - on and the lamb
You de-creed I should be what I am;
Would it spoil some vast e-ter-nal plan, If I were a wealthy man?

It Might As Well Rain Until September

Words and Music by
GERRY GOFFIN and CAROLE KING

Flute/Clarinet or Violin/Strings
Ballad/Pops (Medium-Fast)

The wea-ther here has been as nice as it can be,
Al-though it does-n't real-ly mat-ter much to me;
For all the fun I'll have while you're so far a-way,
It might as well rain un-til Sep-tem-ber.

I don't need sun-ny skies for things I have to do,
'Cause I stay home the whole day long and think of you;
As far as I'm con-cerned each day's a rain-y day,
So it might as well rain un-til Sep-tem-ber.

My friends look for-ward to their pic-nics on the beach:
Yes, ev-'ry-bo-dy

© 1962 & 1989 Screen Gems-EMI Music Inc, USA
Sub-published by Screen Gems-EMI Music Ltd, London WC2H 0EA

Lean On Me

Words and Music
by BILL WITHERS

Violin/Strings
Rock (Medium)

Some - times in our lives ——— we all have pain, ———
Please swal - low your pride ——— if I have things ———
If there is a load ——— you have to bear ———

we all have sor - row. But if we are wise, ———
you need to bor - row, for no one can fill ———
that you can't car - ry, I'm right up the road. ———

we know that there's ——— al - ways to - mor - row. ⎫
those of your needs ——— that you won't let show. ⎬ Lean on
I'll share your load ——— if you just call me. ⎭

me when you're not strong ——— and I'll be your friend, ———

I'll help you car - ry on,

for it won't be long ——— 'til I'm gon - na need ———

some-bo-dy 'to lean ——— on. ——— [1.] lean ——— on. ——— [2.] Just

To Coda ⊕

© 1972 Interior Music Corp, USA
World Excluding USA and Canada U A Music International Inc, USA
Used by Permission   All Rights Reserved

Light My Fire

Words and Music
by THE DOORS

Jazz Organ/Organ 2
Ballad/Pops (Medium-Fast)

© 1967 & 1989 Doors Music Co
All rights for the United Kingdom, Northern Ireland and the Republic of Ireland
controlled by Rondor Music (London) Ltd, London SW6 4TW

2.

The time to hes - i - tate is

through, No time to wal - low in the mire,

Try now we can on - ly lose, And our love be-come a fune-ral

pyre, Come on ba - by, light my fire,

Come on ba-by light my fire,———— Try to set the night on

fire,———— Try to set the night on fire,————

Try to set the night on fire,———— Try to set the night on

fire.——————————

Love Letters

Words by EDWARD HEYMAN
Music by VICTOR YOUNG

Trombone/Trumpet/Brass
Ballad/Pops (Medium Slow)

© 1945 & 1989 Famous Music Corp, USA
Famous Chappell, London W1Y 3FA

Love Of The Common People

Words and Music by
JOHN HURLEY and RONNIE WILKINS

Trombone/Trumpet or Jazz Organ
Rock or 8-beat (Medium)

© 1968 & 1989 Tree Pub Co Inc, USA
Sub-published by EMI Music Publishing Ltd, London WC2H 0EA/Westminster Music Ltd, 19/20 Poland Street, London W1V 1LB

Smiles from the heart of a fam - i - ly man.——

Dad -dy's gon - na buy you a dream to cling to,——

Ma - ma's gon - na love you just as much as she can,——

1. G
And she can.——

2. G
'Cause we're can.——

Verse 2.　It's a good thing you don't have bus fare;
It would fall through the hole in your pocket and you'd lose it in the snow on the ground.
You got to walk into town, to find a job.
Tryin' to keep your hands warm.
When the hole in your shoe lets the snow come through and chills you to the bone.
Now you'd better go home where it's warm.
Where you can live in the love . . . (Chorus)

Verse 3.　Living on a dream ain't easy,
But the closer the knit the tighter the fit and the chills stays away.
You take 'em in the stride for the family pride,
You know that faith is your foundation
And with a whole lot of love and a warm conversation, but don't forget to pray.
Making it strong where you belong,
And we're living in the love . . . (Chorus)

Mandy

Words and Music by
RICHARD KERR and SCOTT ENGLISH

Trumpet/Brass
Ballad/Pops or Bossa Nova (Medium)

© 1971 & 1989 Screen Gems-EMI Music Ltd, London WC2H 0EA/Chappell Music Ltd, London W1Y 3FA

Mexican Hat Dance

Adapted and Arranged
by ROGER EVANS

Trumpet/Brass or Violin/Strings
Waltz (Medium-Fast)
(Add Duet/Counter Melody/Auto Harmonize)

© 1989 International Music Publications, Woodford Green, Essex IG8 8HN

Misty

Words by JOHNNY BURKE
Music by ERROLL GARNER

Jazz Organ/Organ 2 or Trumpet
Ballad/Pops (Slow)

Look at me, I'm as help-less as a kit-ten up a

tree And I feel like I'm cling-ing to a cloud, I

can't ——— un-der-stand ——— I get mist - y just hold - ing your

hand. ————————————— Walk my

way and a thou-sand vi - o - lins be-gin to

play, Or it might be the sound of your hel - lo, That

mu ——— sic I hear ——— I get mist - y, the mo - ment you're

© 1954, 1955 & 1989 Vernon Music Corp, USA
Warner Chappell Music Ltd, London W1Y 3FA

Moonlight (Clair de Lune)

Music by CLAUDE DEBUSSY
New Arrangement
by ROGER EVANS

Organ/Flute or Vibes
Slow Rock or 6-beat (Slow) or play with rhythm switched off
(Add Arpeggio/Variation)

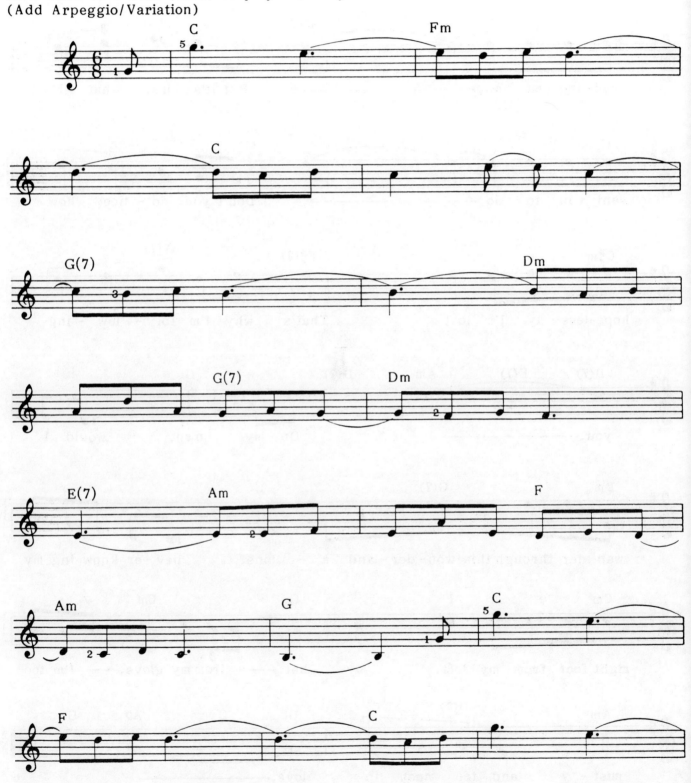

© 1989 International Music Publications, Woodford Green, Essex IG8 8HN

103

Moon River

Words by JOHNNY MERCER
Music by HENRY MANCINI

Violin/Strings or Trumpet
Waltz (Slow)
(Add Variation)

© 1961 & 1989 Famous Music Corp, USA
Famous Chappell, London W1Y 3FA

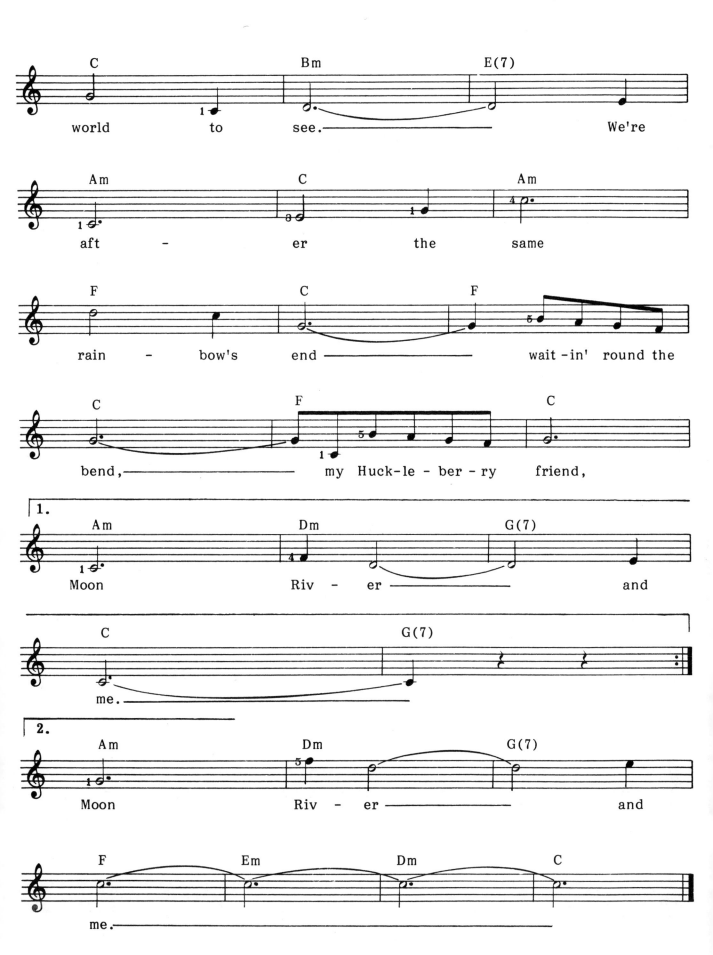

The More I See You

Words by MACK GORDON
Music by HARRY WARREN

Organ/Organ 1
Ballad/Pops or Bossa Nova (Medium-Fast)

© 1945 & 1989 Twentieth Century Music Corp, USA
Rights controlled by Bregman, Vocco & Conn Inc, USA
Chappell Music Ltd, London W1Y 3FA

Mr. Tambourine Man

Words and Music
by BOB DYLAN

Organ
Ballad/Pops (Medium-Fast)
(Add Arpeggio/Variation)

©1964 (Unp) by W Witmark & Sons in the USA
© 1965 & 1989 M Witmark & Sons under Universal Copyright Convention
Warner Chappell Music Ltd, London W1Y 3FA

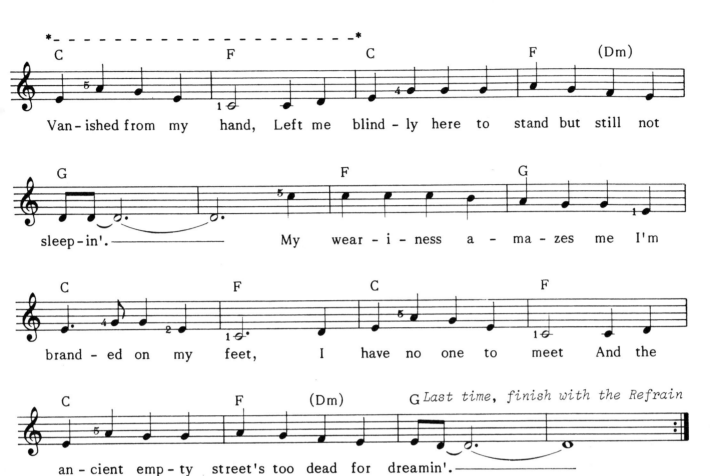

Van-ished from my hand, Left me blind-ly here to stand but still not sleep-in'.———— My wear-i-ness a-ma-zes me I'm brand-ed on my feet, I have no one to meet And the an-cient emp-ty street's too dead for dreamin'.————

- - - - Repeat these bars to fit in extra lyrics for verses 2, 3 & 4.

Verse 3. Take me on a trip upon your magic swirlin' ship
My senses have been stripped, my hands can't feel to grip,
My toes too numb to step, wait only for my boot heels to be wanderin'.
I'm ready to go anywhere, I'm ready for to fade
Into my own parade, cast your dancin' spell my way
I promise to go under it.

Verse 3. Though you might hear laughin' spinnin' swingin' madly across the sun
It's not aimed at anyone, it's just escapin' on the run
And but for the sky there are no fences facin'.
And if you hear vague traces, of skippin' reels of rhyme
To your tambourine in time, it's just a ragged clown behind,
I wouldn't pay it any mind, it's just a shadow
You're seein' that he's chasin'.

Verse 4. Then take me disappearin' through the smoke rings of my mind
Down the foggy ruins of time, far past the frozen leaves,
The haunted frightened trees, out to the windy beach
Far from the twisted reach of crazy sorrow.
Yes, to dance beneath the diamond sky, with one hand wavin' free
Silhouetted by the sea, circled by the circus sands
With all memory and fate, driven deep beneath the waves.
Let me forget about today until tomorrow.

Repeat refrain.

My Way

French Words by GILLES THIBAUT
English Lyrics by PAUL ANKA
Music by CLAUDE FRANCOIS and JACQUES REVAUX

Trumpet/Brass or Organ
Ballad/Pops or Swing (Medium-Slow)

© 1967 & 1989 Ste des Nelles Editions Eddie Barclay, France and Editions Jeune Musique, France
Intersong Music Ltd, London W1Y 3FA

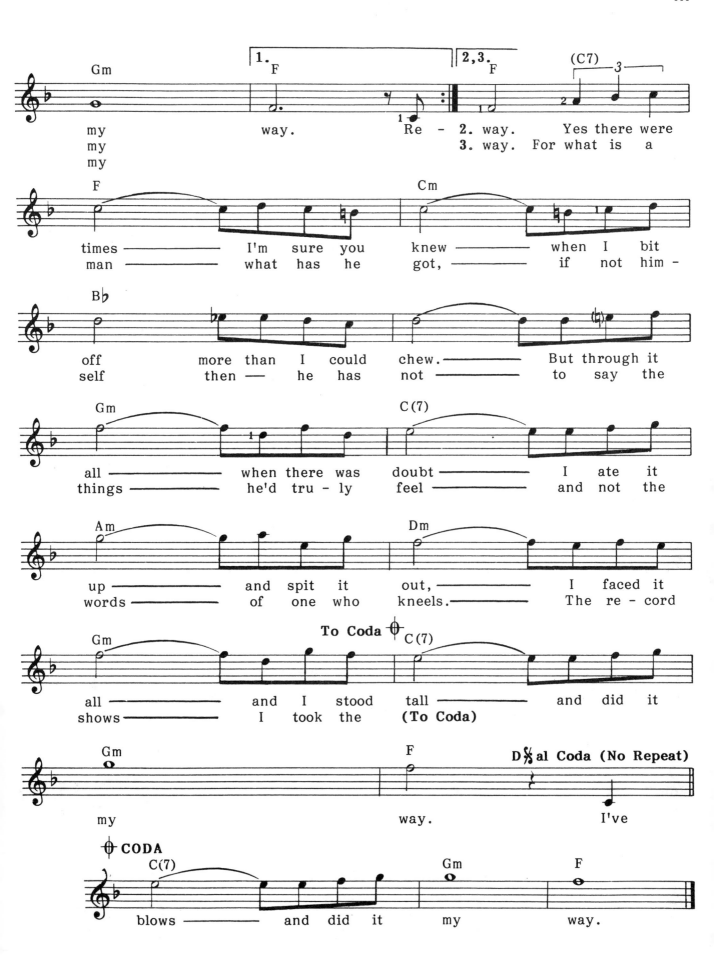

Never Can Say Goodbye

Words and Music
by CLIFTON DAVIS

Violin/Strings
Disco or Rock (Medium)

© 1970 & 1989 Jobete Music Co Inc,
Jobete Music (UK) Ltd, Tudor House, 35 Gresse Street, London W1P 1PN

Verse 3. (I keep) thinkin' that our problems soon are all gonna work out,
But there's that same unhappy feelin', there's that anguish, there's that doubt.
It's the same old dizzy hang-up, can't do with you or without.
Tell me why, is it so? Don't wanna let you go.

Nights In White Satin

Words and Music
by JUSTIN HAYWARD

Organ/Organ 1 (Optional: Change to Flute later)
Slow Rock or 6-beat (Slow)
(Add Stereo Chorus/Stereo Symphonic)

© 1967 & 1989 Tyler Music Ltd, 19/20 Poland Street, London W1V 3DD

Night-Time In Moscow

Adapted and Arranged
by ROGER EVANS

Trumpet/Trombone or Clarinet
Swing (Medium Fast)

* Key change to Am, Play B (♮) instead of B♭ from here on.

© 1989 International Music Publications, Woodford Green, Essex IG8 8HN

Nobody Does It Better

Words by CAROLE BAYER SAGER
Music by MARVIN HAMLISCH

Flute or Organ
Ballad/Pops (Medium-Slow)

© 1977 & 1989 DANJAQ S.A.
All rights controlled by United Artists Music Co Inc and Unart Music Corp,
All rights of United Artists Music Co Inc and Unart Music Corp assigned to SBK Catalogue Partnership
All rights administered by SBK U Catalog and SBK Unart Catalog
Used by Permission

keep - in' all my se - crets safe to - night.
how d'you learn to do the things you

do? And no - bo - dy does it

bet - ter makes me feel sad for the

rest. No - bo - dy does it

half as good as you. Ba - by, ba - by,

ba - by you're the best.

Ba - by, ba - by, ba - by you're the

best.

O Danny Boy

Adapted and Arranged
by ROGER EVANS

Organ or Flute
Ballad/Pops (Medium)
(Arpeggio/Variation)

O Dan - ny Boy, the pipes, the pipes are

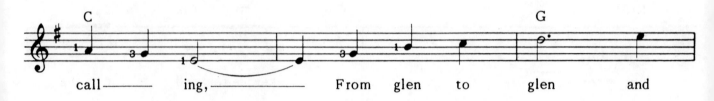

call——ing,———— From glen to glen and

o'er the moun-tain side.——————— The sum-mer's gone, and

all the leaves are fall——ing,———— It's you, it's

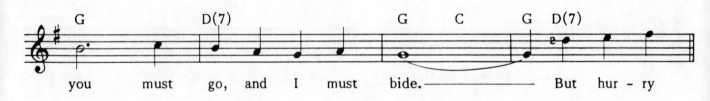

you must go, and I must bide.————— But hur - ry

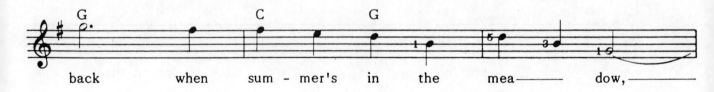

back when sum - mer's in the mea——dow,———

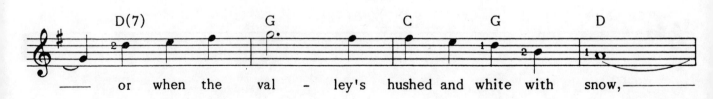

—— or when the val - ley's hushed and white with snow,———

© 1989 International Music Publications, Woodford Green, Essex IG8 8HN

121

One Moment In Time

Words and Music by
ALBERT HAMMOND and JOHN BETTIS

Violin/Strings or Organ
Ballad/Pops (Medium)

Each day I live I want to be a day to give the best of me. I'm on-ly one but not a- lone, my fin-est day is yet un-known. I broke my

heart / be for ev-'ry gain, / the ve-ry best, to taste the sweet / I want it all, yet through it all / now lay the chance I faced the / here in my

pain, / less, I rise and fall / I've laid the plans, yet through it all / now lay the chance this much re- / here in my

- mains. / hands. I want / Give me } one mo-ment in time When I'm

more than I thought I could be. When all of my dreams are a

© 1988 & 1989 Empire Music Limited/Albert Hammond Inc/Warner Chappell Music Limited, London W1Y 3FA

Over The Rainbow

Words by E Y HARBURG
Music by HAROLD ARLEN

Trumpet/Brass or Jazz Organ
Ballad/Pops (Medium-Slow)

© 1938, 1939 (Renewed 1966, 1967) & 1989 Metro-Goldwyn-Mayer Inc, USA
All rights controlled by Leo Feist, Inc
All rights of Leo Feist Inc, Assigned to SBK Catalogue Partnership
All rights administered by SBK Feist Catalog
Used by Permission

Over The Waves

Music by JUVENTINO ROSAS
Adapted and Arranged
by ROGER EVANS

Flute or Clarinet
Waltz (Medium)
(Add Variation)

© 1989 International Music Publications, Woodford Green, Essex IG8 8HN

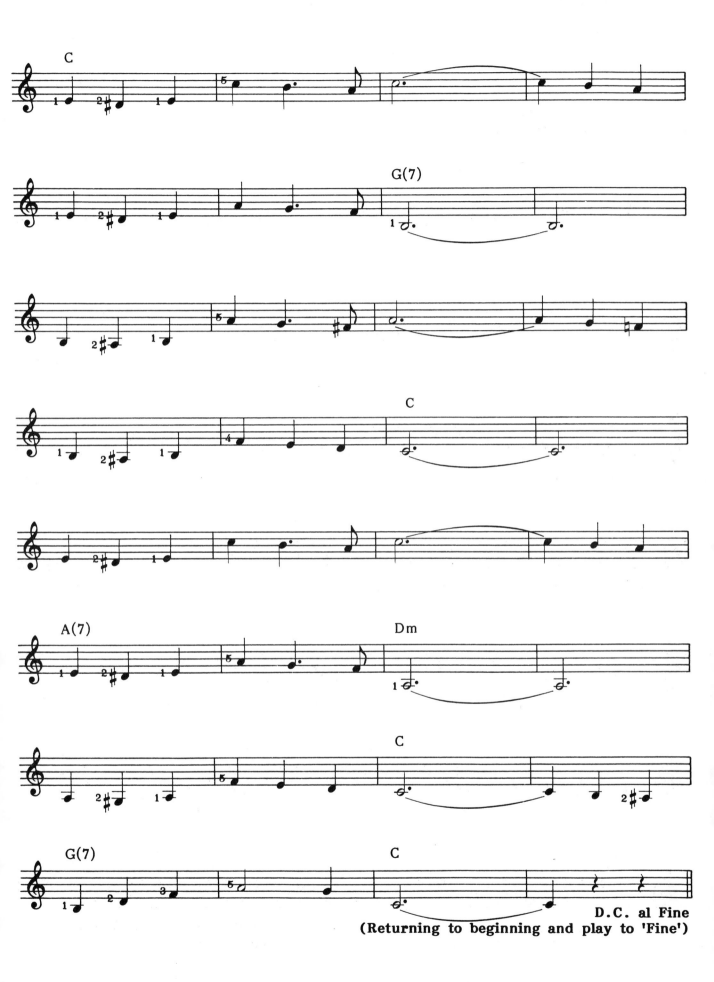

D.C. al Fine
(Returning to beginning and play to 'Fine')

Paloma Blanca

Words and Music
by J BOUWENS

Trumpet/Brass or Clarinet
March or Country (Medium-Fast)

Instrumental (Optional) ———

When the sun shines on the moun - tains ———

And the night is on the run ———

It's a new day, It's a new way ———

And I fly up to the sun. *Instrumental* ———

I can feel the
had my

morn - ing sun - light, ——— I can smell the new-mown
share of los - ing, ——— For they locked me on a

© 1975 & 1989 Witch/Veronica Music, Holland
Noon Music Ltd, London

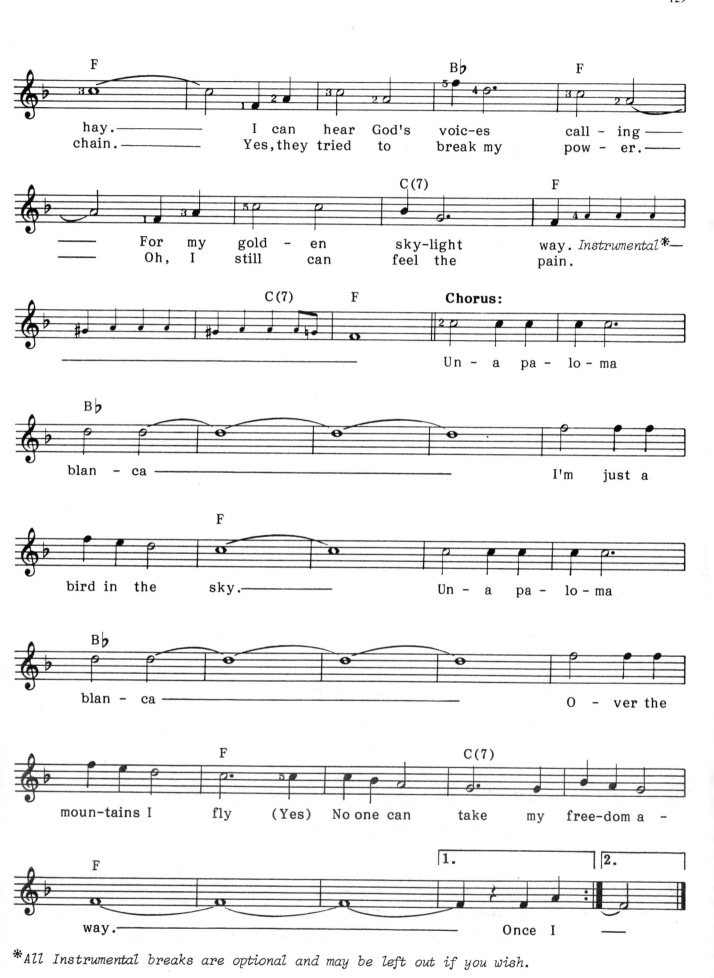

hay. —————— I can hear God's voic-es call - ing ——
chain. —————— Yes, they tried to break my pow - er. ——

—— For my gold - en sky-light way. *Instrumental**——
—— Oh, I still can feel the pain.

Un - a pa - lo - ma

Chorus:

blan - ca —————————————————— I'm just a

bird in the sky. ————— Un - a pa - lo - ma

blan - ca ————————————————— O - ver the

moun-tains I fly (Yes) No one can take my free-dom a -

way. ————————————— Once I ——

1. **2.**

All Instrumental breaks are optional and may be left out if you wish.

Piano In The Dark

Words and Music by BRENDA RUSSELL,
JEFF HULL and SCOTT CUTLER

Flute or Electric Piano/Piano*
Bossa Nova or Ballad/Pops (Medium)
(*Add Stereo Chorus/Stereo Symphonic)

© 1988 & 1989 WB Music Corp, Rutland Road Music, Dwarf Village Music & Colgems-EMI Music Inc
Screen Gems-EMI Music Ltd, London WC2H 0EA/Warner Chappell Music Ltd, London W1Y 3FA

Remember The Night (Danube Waves)

Music by JAN IVANOVICI
Adapted and Arranged
by ROGER EVANS

Flute/Clarinet or Trumpet
Waltz (Medium-Fast) or Slow Rock
(Add Arpeggio/Variation)

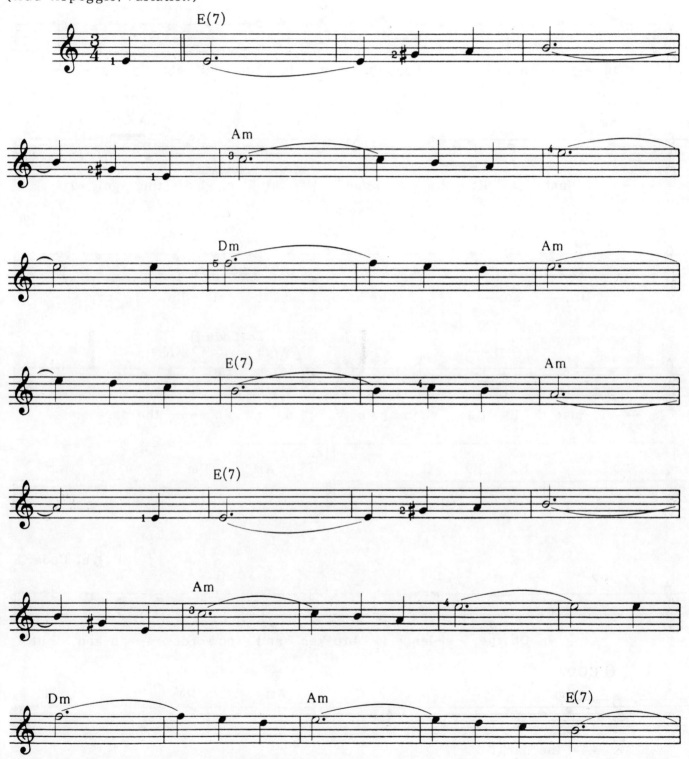

© 1989 International Music Publications, Woodford Green, Essex IG8 8HN

133

Satisfaction (I Can't Get No)

Words by Music by
MICK JAGGER and KEITH RICHARDS

Jazz Organ/Organ 2 or Violin/Strings
8-beat, Rock or Disco (Medium-Fast)

© 1965, 1974 & 1989 Westminster Music Ltd/Abkco Music Inc, London W1V 3DD

tell-in' me more and more a-bout some use-less in-form-
white — my shirts can be, Well, he can't be a man, 'cause
try-in' to make some girl. Who tells me, ba-by better come back

-a-tion, sup-posed to fire my im-a-gin-a-tion.
he does-n't smoke the same cig-a-rettes as me.
la-ter next week,'cause you see I'm on a los-ing streak.
I can't

get no, Oh, no, no, no, Hey,hey,

1,2.

hey —— that's what I say. ——

3.

I can't get no, I can't get no,

I can't get no sat-is-fac-tion,

No sat-is-fac-tion, No sat-is-fac-tion

Repeat and fade

No sat-is-fac-tion.

Saving All My Love For You

Words by GERRY GOFFIN
Music by MICHAEL MASSER

Violin/Strings or Organ
Slow Rock (Medium-Slow)

© 1978 & 1989 Screen Gems-EMI Music Inc and Prince Street Music
Warner Chappell Music Ltd, London WC2H 0EA

Secret Love

Words by PAUL FRANCIS WEBSTER
Music by SAMMY FAIN

Violin/Strings
Slow Rock or Swing (Medium)

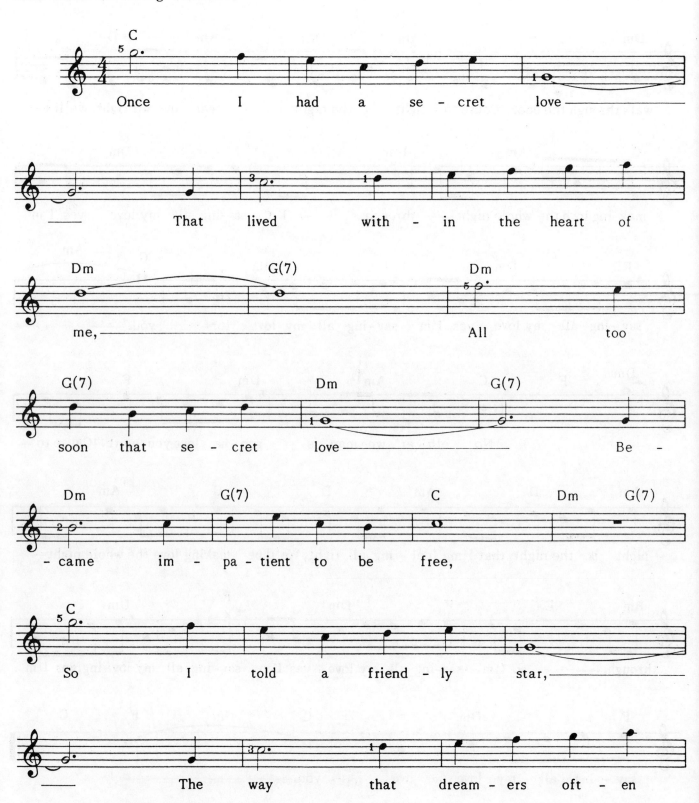

© 1953 & 1989 Remick Music Corp, USA
Warner Chappell Music Ltd, London W1Y 3FA

Skye Boat Song

Adapted and Arranged
by ROGER EVANS

Flute/Clarinet or Accordion
Waltz (Medium-Slow)
(Add Arpeggio/Variation)

"Speed bon-nie boat, like a bird on the wing, On - ward!" the sail - ors cry. _____ "Car - ry the lad that's born to be King, O - ver the sea to Skye." _____ Loud the winds howl, loud the waves roar, Thun - der clouds rend the

© 1989 International Music Publications, Woodford Green, Essex IG8 8HN

Smoke Gets In Your Eyes

Words by OTTO HARBACH
Music by JEROME KERN

Trumpet (Change to Violin or Strings later)
Ballad/Pops (Medium-Not too fast)

© 1933 & 1989 Jerome Kern, USA
Published T B Harms Co, USA
Redwood Music Ltd, London NW1 8BD/Polygram Music Publishing Ltd, London W6 0RA

Snowbird

Words and Music
by GENE MacLELLAN

© 1970 & 1989 Beechwood Music of Canada, Canada
Ardmore & Beechwood Ltd, London WC2H 0EA

Spanish Eyes

Words by CHARLES SINGLETON and EDDIE SNYDER
Music by BERT KAEMPFERT

Trumpet/Brass
Bossa Nova (Medium)
(Second time through add Duet/Counter Melody)

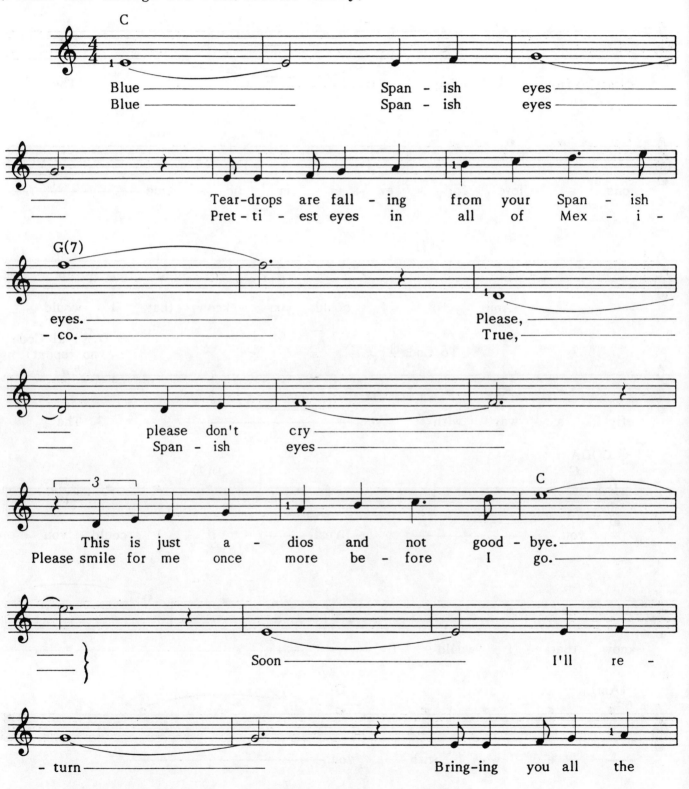

© 1965 & 1989 Editions Bert Kaempfert, Germany. Copyright for the World
outside Germany, Austria and Switzerland assigned to: Roosevelt Music Co Inc, USA
Carlin Music Corp, London W1X 2LR

Stairway To Heaven

Words and Music by
JIMMY PAGE and ROBERT PLANT

Jazz Organ/Organ 2 or Flute
8-beat or Rock (Slow)
(Add Arpeggio/Variation)

© 1972 & 1989 Superhype Publishing, USA
Warner Chappell Music Ltd, London W1Y 3FA

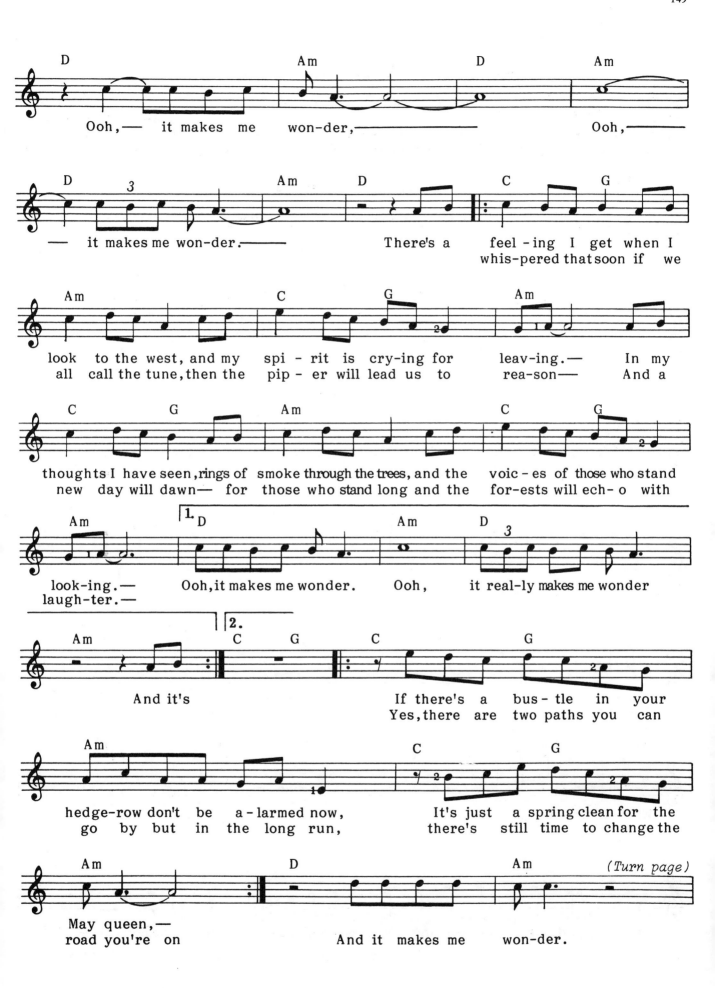

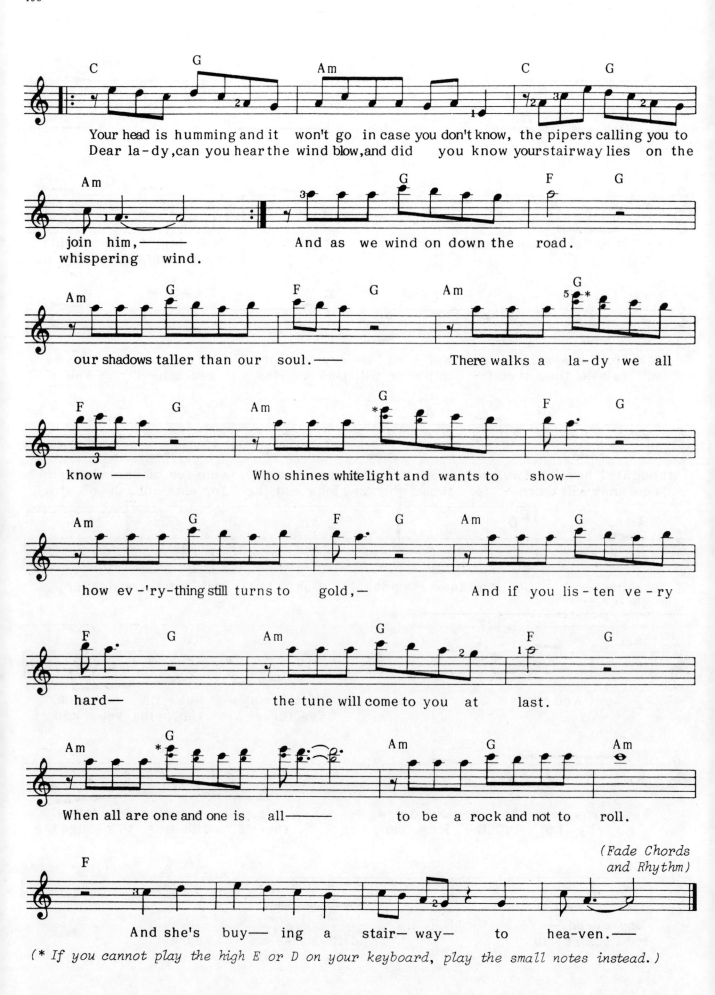

Your head is humming and it won't go in case you don't know, the pipers calling you to
Dear la-dy, can you hear the wind blow, and did you know your stairway lies on the

join him, ——— And as we wind on down the road.
whispering wind.

our shadows taller than our soul. —— There walks a la-dy we all

know ——— Who shines white light and wants to show—

how ev-'ry-thing still turns to gold, — And if you lis-ten ve-ry

hard— the tune will come to you at last.

When all are one and one is all——— to be a rock and not to roll.

(Fade Chords and Rhythm)

And she's buy—— ing a stair—way— to hea-ven.——

(* If you cannot play the high E or D on your keyboard, play the small notes instead.)

Sloop John B

Adapted and Arranged
by ROGER EVANS

Trumpet/Brass or Vibes
Bossa Nova (Medium)

1. We came on the Sloop John B, My old grand dad-dy and
hoist up the John B sails See how the main sail's

me, All a-round Nas-sau Town We — did roam.
set, Send for the Captain a - shore Let me go home.

—— Drinking all night —— Got in a fight, —— I
—— Let me go home —— Let me go home, —— I

feel so broke up, I want to go home. Chorus: So
feel so broke up, I want to go home.

Last time only

I feel so broke up, I want to go home. ——

Verse 2. The first mate he got drunk
Broke up the people's trunk
Constable had to come and take him away.
Sheriff John Stone, please leave me alone
I feel so broke up I want to go home.

Chorus.

Verse 3. The cook he got the fits,
He ate up all of my grits.
Then he took and ate up all of my corn
Leave me alone, I want to go home,
This is the worst trip I've ever been on.

Chorus.

© 1989 International Music Publications, Woodford Green, Essex IG8 8HN

Stay With Me (Jazz Samba)

Music by ROGER EVANS

Trombone/Trumpet or Saxophone
Samba (Medium)
(Add Variation)

© 1989 International Music Publications, Woodford Green, Essex IG8 8HN

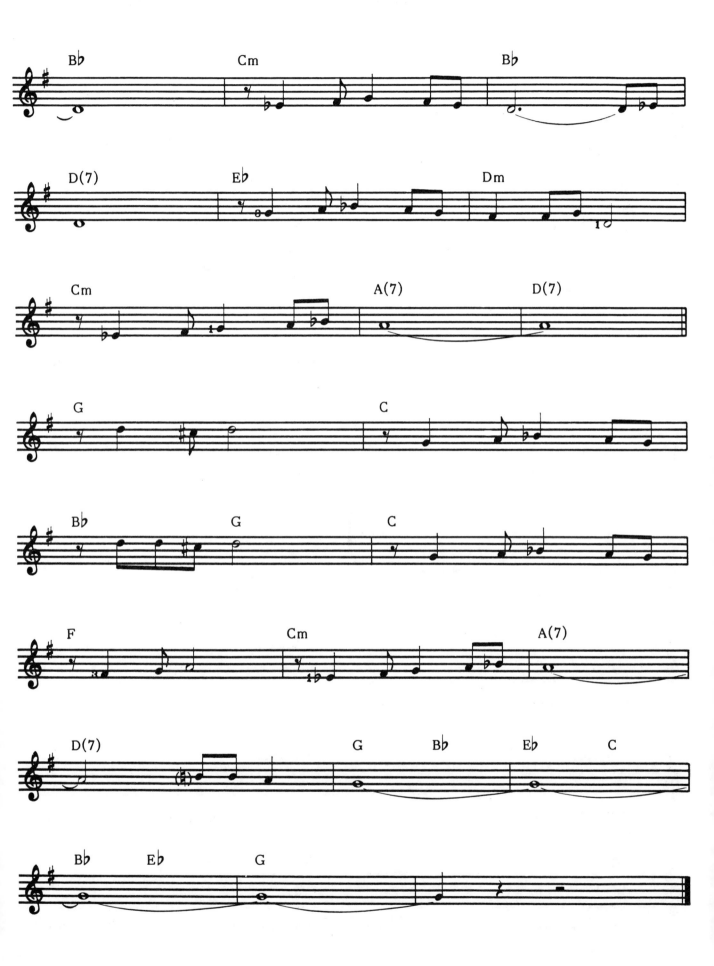

The Summer Knows (Theme From 'Summer Of 42')

Words by MARILYN and ALAN BERGMAN
Music by MICHEL LEGRAND

Piano/Electric Piano or Violin/Strings
Ballad/Pops (Slow)
(Add Arpeggio or Variation)

© 1971 & 1989 WB Music Corp, USA
Warner Chappell Music Ltd, London W1Y 3FA

moon   to   wait   and the   sun   to   lin – ger,

Twists   the   world   'round her   sum – mer   fin – ger,

Lets   you   see   the   won – der of   it   all,   And

if you've learned——your   les-son well,   There's lit – tle more———— for

*(Key Change)

her   to   tell,   One   last   car – ess,———————— it's

1. Gm

time   to dress   for   fall.————————   The

2. Gm

fall.—————————   (Instrumental ————————————)

* **Note:** This music changes key from G minor with two flats (B♭ and E♭) in the key signature, to G (major) with one sharp (F♯) in the key signature. Then it changes back again to G minor.

Summertime

Words by DuBOSE HEYWARD
Music by GEORGE GERSHWIN

Flute or Clarinet
Bossa Nova (Medium)
(Add Stereo Chorus or Stereo Symphonic)

© 1935 & 1989 Gershwin Publishing Corp, USA
Chappell Music Ltd, London W1Y 3FA

Swinging On A Star

Words by JOHNNY BURKE
Music by JIMMY VAN HEUSEN

Trombone/Trumpet or Clarinet
Ballad/Pops or Swing (Medium)

(See next page for optional "intro")

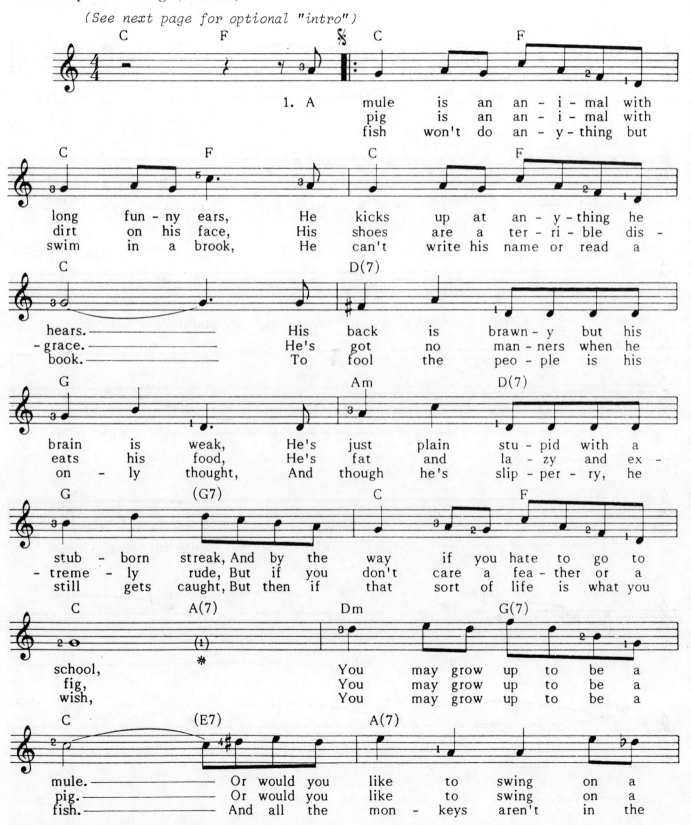

Hold down note and change fingers

© 1944 & 1989 Burke and Van Heusen Inc, USA
Chappell Morris Ltd, London W1Y 3FA

★ *Hold down note and change fingers*

Take Good Care Of My Baby

Words and Music by
GERRY GOFFIN and CAROLE KING

Electric Piano or Trumpet/Brass
Ballad/Pops or Rock (Medium-Fast)

© 1961 & 1989 Screen Gems-EMI Music Inc, USA
Sub-published by Screen Gems-EMI Music Ltd, London WC2H 0EA

Tell It To My Heart

Words and Music by
ERNIE GOLD and SETH SWIRSKY

© 1987 & 1989 Gold Joint Music/Chappell & Co Inc/November Nights Music
Chappell Music Ltd, London W1Y 3FA/Warner Chappell Music Ltd, London W1Y 3FA

There's A Kind Of Hush

Words and Music by
LES REED and GEOFF STEPHENS

Piano/Electric Guitar or Jazz Organ
Ballad/Pops (Medium-Fast)

© 1966 & 1989 Donna Music Ltd, London WC2H 0EA

Tonight I Celebrate My Love

Words and Music by
MICHAEL MASSER and GERRY GOFFIN

Flute/Clarinet
Ballad/Pops (Slow)
(Add Arpeggio/Variation)

© 1983 & 1989 Screen Gems-EMI Music Inc/Almo Music Corp/Print Street Music (USA)
Sub-published by Screen Gems-EMI Ltd, London WC2H 0EA/Rondor Music (London) Ltd, London SW6 4TW

The Tracks Of My Tears

Words and Music by WILLIAM "SMOKEY" ROBINSON,
WARREN MOORE and MARV TARPLIN

Organ or Trumpet
Rock or Ballad/Pops (Medium-Not too fast)

© 1965, 1967 & 1989 Jobete Music Co Inc, USA
Jobete Music (UK) Ltd, Tudor House, 35 Gresse Street, London W1P 1PN

tears.
tears.   I need

you   need —————— you.
you   need —————— you.

My smile is my make - up I

wear since my break - up with you.   Ba - by, take a

good   look at my face ——————— you'll see my

smile —————— looks out of place. ——————— If you look

clo - ser it's ea - sy to trace   the tracks of my

tears,   Oh. ————————————————

True Love

Words and Music by COLE PORTER

Violin/Strings or Clarinet/Flute
Waltz (Slow)
(Add Arpeggio/Variation)

© 1955 (unpub) 1956 & 1989 Buxton Hill Music Corp, USA
Chappell Music Ltd, London W1Y 3FA

Try To Remember

Words by TOM JONES
Music by HARVEY SCHMIDT

Clarinet/Flute
Waltz (Medium-Slow)
(Add Variation)

Try to re - mem - ber the

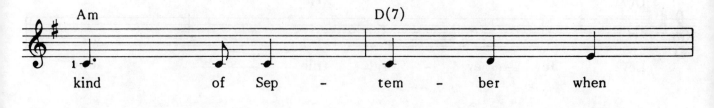

kind of Sep - tem - ber when

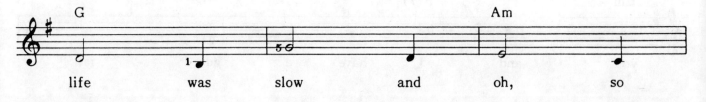

life was slow and oh, so

mel - low.—— Try to re - mem - ber the

kind of Sep - tem - ber when grass was

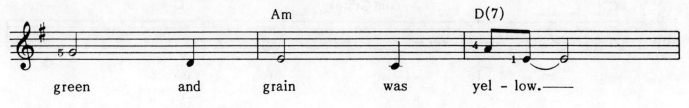

green and grain was yel - low.——

Try to re - mem - ber the

© 1960 & 1989 Tom Jones and Harvey Schmidt
Chappell & Co Inc, New York, NY, Owner of publication and allied rights throughout the world
Chappell Music Ltd, London W1Y 3FA

Up Where We Belong

Words by WILL JENNINGS
Music by BUFFY SAINTE-MARIE and JACK NITZSCHE

Trumpet/Brass
Ballad/Pops (Medium)

© 1982 & 1989 Famous Music Corp and Ensign Music Corp, USA
Famous Chappell, London W1Y 3FA

(* If your keyboard has a 'Transposer,' you could use it to change Key at this point by setting it to +1 or C♯.)

We'll Meet Again

Words and Music by
ROSS PARKER and **HUGHIE CHARLES**

Trombone/Trumpet/Brass
Swing or Slow Rock (Medium)

© 1939 & 1989 for all countries by Dash Music Co Ltd, London W1V 5TZ

What A Wonderful World

Words and Music by
GEORGE DAVID WEISS and BOB THIELE

Trumpet/Brass
Ballad/Pops or Slow Rock (Medium)

© 1967 & 1989 Herald Square Music Co, USA
Carlin Music Corp, London W1X 2LR

179

What's Love Got To Do With It

Words and Music by
GRAHAM LYLE and TERRY BRITTEN

Jazz Organ/Organ 2 or Saxophone
Rock (Medium)

© 1984 & 1989 Good Single Ltd, and Chappell Music Ltd
Rondor Music (London) Ltd, London SW6 4TW/Chappell Music Ltd, London W1Y 3FA

heart can be bro-ken? It

heart can be bro - ken?—— I've been tak-ing on a

new di - rec-tion

but I have—— to say,——

I've been thinking about my own pro - tec-tion, it scares me to feel this

way. Oh—— what's love—— got to do, got to do with it,

What's love—— but a { sec - ond-hand e - mo - tion?——
sweet old fash-ioned no - tion?—— }

What's love—— got to do, got to do with it,

Who needs a heart when a heart can be bro - ken, heart can be bro - ken.——

(Repeat and Fade)

When I Need You

Words by CAROLE BAYER SAGER
Music by ALBERT HAMMOND

Violin/Strings
Waltz (Medium)

©1976 & 1989 Begonia Melodies Inc, Unichappell Music Inc and Albert Hammond Music, USA
April Music Ltd, London W1P 1DA/Chappell Music Ltd, London W1Y 3FA

Where Do I Begin (Theme from 'Love Story')

Words by CARL SIGMAN
Music by FRANCIS LAI

Piano (Change to Violin or Strings later)
Bossa Nova (Medium)
(Add Stereo Chorus/Stereo Symphonic)

Am

Where do I be - gin ⎯⎯⎯ to tell the sto - ry of how
How long does it last? ⎯⎯⎯ Can love be mea - sured by the

E(7)

great a love can be, ⎯⎯⎯ The sweet love sto - ry that is
ho - urs in a day? ⎯⎯⎯ I have no an - swers now, but

Am   **F**

old - er than the sea, ⎯⎯⎯ The sim - ple truth a - bout the
this much I can say: ⎯⎯⎯ I know I'll need her 'til the

E(7)   **To Coda**

love she brings to me? ⎯⎯⎯
stars all burn a - way ⎯⎯⎯ Where do I

Am   *(Change to Violin or Strings)*

start? ⎯⎯⎯

With her first hel - lo ⎯⎯⎯ she gave a mean - ing to this

E(7)

emp - ty world of mine; ⎯⎯⎯ There'd nev - er be an - oth - er

© 1970, 1971 & 1989 Famous Music Corp, USA
Famous Chappell, London W1Y 3FA

love, an-oth-er time: ——————— She came in-to my life and

made the liv-ing fine. ——————— She fills my

heart, ——————— She fills my heart ——— with ve-ry

spe-cial things,—with an-gel songs, — with wild im - ag-in-ings.—She fills my

soul ——— with so much love, That an-y-where I go ——— I'm nev-er

lone - ly.——With her a - long, ——— who could be lone-ly?— I reach for her

hand,——— It's al-ways there.———————

(Change back to Piano)   **D. %̸ al Coda** ⊕

⊕ **CODA**

— And she'll be there.———————

A Whiter Shade Of Pale

Words and Music by
KEITH REID and GARY BROOKER

Organ/Organ 1
8-beat or Ballad/Pops (Medium-Slow)

© 1967 & 1989 Westminster Music Ltd, 19/20 Poland Street, London W1V 3DD

Will You Love Me Tomorrow

Words and Music by
GERRY GOFFIN and **CAROLE KING**

Organ or Flute/Clarinet
Rock or Ballad/Pops (Medium)

© 1960 & 1989 Screen Gems-EMI Music Inc, USA
Sub-published by Screen Gems-EMI Music Ltd, London WC2H 0EA

The Wind Beneath My Wings

Words and Music by
LARRY HENLY and JEFF SILBAR

Violin/Strings or Jazz Organ
Ballad/Pops (Medium-Slow)
(Add Arpeggio/Variation)

1. It must have been cold there in my sha - dow,
2. I was the one with all the glor - y,

to nev-er have sun - light —— on your face.
while you were the one with —— all the strength.

You've been con - tent to let me shine,
On - ly a face with-out a name.

you al - ways walked one step be -
I nev - er once heard you com -

- hind.
- plain.

Did you ev - er know that you're my he - ro,

and ev -'ry - thing I'd like to be?

© 1981 & 1983 Warner House of Music and WB Gold Music Corp
Warner Chappell Music Ltd, London W1Y 3FA

You Don't Have To Say You Love Me

Original Italian Words by V PALLAVICINI
English Lyrics by VICKI WICKHAM and SIMON NAPIER-BELL
Music by P DONAGGIO

Trumpet/Brass or Jazz Organ
Slow Rock (Medium-Slow)

When I said I need-ed you —— You said you would al-ways stay, —— It was-n't me who changed but you, and now you've gone a-way. Don't you see that now you've gone, —— And I'm left here on my own, —— That I have to fol-low you and beg you to come home. You don't have to say you love me, just be close at hand, You don't have to stay for ev-er, I will un-der-stand, Be-

© 1965 & 1989 Edizioni Musical Accordo, Italy
Sub-published by B Feldman & Co Ltd, London WC2H 0EA

You Light Up My Life

Words and Music
by JOE BROOKS

Violin/Strings or Jazz Organ/Organ 2
Waltz (Medium-Slow)
(Add Arpeggio/Variation)

© 1976 & 1989 Big Hill Music, USA
Sub-published by EMI Music Publishing Ltd, London WC2H 0EA

You Needed Me

Words and Music
by RANDY GOODRUM

Trumpet/Brass or Electric Guitar
Ballad/Pops (Medium-Slow)

© 1975, 1978 and 1989 Chappell & Co Inc and Ironside Music, USA
Chappell Music Ltd, London W1Y 3FA

You To Me Are Everything

Words and Music by
KEN GOLD and MICHAEL DENNE

Jazz Organ/Organ 2 or Flute
Rock or Disco (Medium)

I would take the stars out of the sky for you,

stop the rain from fall-ing if you asked me to.

I'd do an-y-thing for you, Your wish is my com-mand,

I could move a moun-tain when your hand is in my hand.

Words can-not ex-press how much you mean to me.
Though you're close to me we seem so far a-part,

There must be some oth-er way to make you see. If it takes my heart and soul you
May-be, giv-en time, you'll have a change of heart. If it takes for-ev-er, girl, then

know I'd pay the price. Ev-'ry-thing that I poss-ess I'd glad-ly sac-ri-fice. Oh
I'm prepared to wait. The day you give your love to me won't be a day too late.

© 1976 & 1989 Screen Gems-EMI Music Ltd, London WC2H 0EA

You'll Never Walk Alone

Words by OSCAR HAMMERSTEIN II
Music by RICHARD RODGERS

Violin/Strings
Ballad/Pops (Medium)

© 1945, 1956 & 1989 T B Harms Co
Chappell Music Ltd, London W1Y 3FA

You're So Vain

Words and Music
by **CARLY SIMON**

Jazz Organ/Organ 2 or Electric Guitar
Ballad/Pops (Medium/Medium-Fast)

© 1972 & 1989 Hackenbush Music, Ltd
Warner Chappell Music Ltd, London W1Y 3FA

they'd be your part— ner, and ⎫
clouds in my cof — fee, and ⎬ You're so —
wife of a close— friend, ⎭

vain You prob-'ly think this song is a-bout—

— you, you're so — vain. I'll

bet you think this song is a-bout — you.— Don't you?—

1.2. Don't you?— **2.** You **3.** Don't you?————
3. Well, I

You're so — vain, you

prob-'ly think this song is a-bout you. You're so —

Repeat and Fade

vain, you prob-'ly think this song is a-bout you.

You've Lost That Lovin' Feelin'

Words and Music by PHIL SPECTOR,
BARRY MANN and CYNTHIA WEIL

Organ or Violin/Strings
Ballad/Pops (Medium-Slow)

1. You nev - er close your eyes an - y
wel - come look in your

more when I kiss your lips
eyes when I reach for you
And there's no
And girl, you're

ten - der - ness like be - fore in your fin - ger - tips.
start - in' to crit - i - cize lit - tle things I do.

You're try - in' hard not to show it, but
It makes me just feel like cry - in', 'cause

ba - by, ba - by, I know it,
ba - by, Some-thing beau-ti - ful's dy - in'.

1.2. You've lost that
3. Bring back that

lov - in' feel - in'.
lov - in' feel - in'.

Woh oh, that lov - in' feel - in'

You've lost that lov - in' feel-in, Now it's gone, gone,

© 1974 & 1989 Screen Gems-EMI Music Inc, USA
Sub-published by Screen Gems-EMI Music Ltd, London WC2H 0EA

gone, Woh oh oh oh.———————— 2. Now there's no

oh. (Instrumental * ————————————) Ba - by, ba - by, I'd get

down on my knees for you. (Instrumental ————————————)

If that would make you love me like you used to do. (Instrumental ——

———————————) We had a love, a love you don't find ev - er - y

day. (Instrumental ————————————) So don't, don't

don't, don't let it slip a - way.————————————

oh. (Instrumental ————————————)

* All Instrumentals optional

Ask your music dealer for these easy music books by Roger Evans:

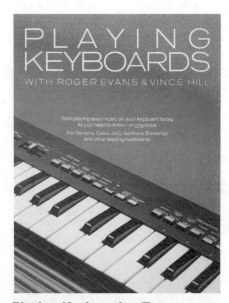

Playing Keyboards - Tutor
All you need to know to play easy keyboard music — in one book! With this easy book you can start playing popular tunes on your keyboard in minutes — even if you know nothing about music before you begin.
Tunes to play include: Flashdance ...What A Feeling, Hello, Send In The Clowns — and many more.
Plus there's a matching cassette!

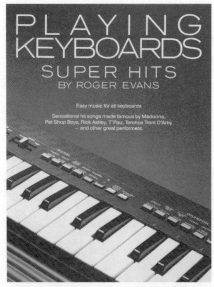

Playing Keyboards - Super Hits
Sensational hit songs and classic hits made famous by Rick Astley, Pet Shop Boys, T'Pau, Madonna, Terence Trent D'Arby and other great performers.
Features: Always On My Mind, China In Your Hand, When I Fall In Love, Ev'ry Time We Say Good-bye, Stand By Me, Never Gonna Give You Up, When A Man Loves A Woman — and many more.

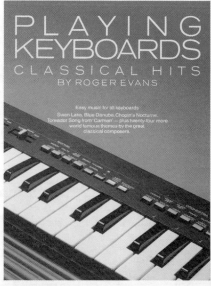

Playing Keyboards - Classical Hits
Impress your family and friends with this glittering collection of popular classical music.
This entertaining book features classical masterpieces by Bach, Beethoven, Chopin, Tchaikovsky and other great composers — all specially selected and made easy for keyboards by Roger Evans.
Includes: Swan Lake, Blue Danube, Chopin's Nocturne — and many more.

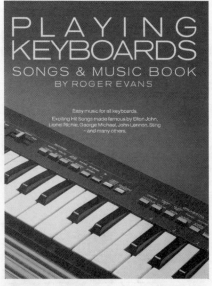

Playing Keyboards - Songs & Music Book 1
An exciting collection of hit songs and popular music. This enjoyable book features songs made famous by such great performers as George Michael, Elton John, Lionel Richie, Sting, John Lennon and many others.
Includes: Careless Whisper, Every Breath You Take, Three Times A Lady, Imagine — plus many more.

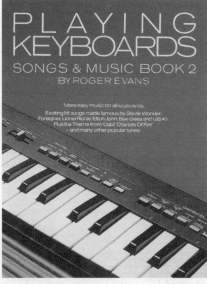

Playing Keyboards - Songs & Music Book 2
Exciting hit songs by Elton John, Stevie Wonder, Lionel Richie, John Lennon, Bee Gees and other outstanding artists — plus many popular keyboard tunes.
Features: I Just Called To Say I Love You, Say You Say Me, Nikita, I Want To Know What Love Is, Memory (from 'Cats'), You've Got A Friend — and many more.

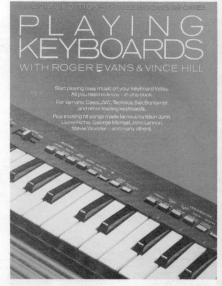

Playing Keyboards - Special 3-in-1 Edition
The best-selling Playing Keyboards tutor book, plus Playing Keyboards Songs & Music Books 1 and 2 together in one super book.
All you need to know to play easy keyboard music — plus all of the hit songs and popular music from two great Playing Keyboards song-books. 50 tunes to play, all specially arranged by Roger Evans.

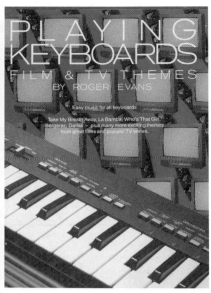

Playing Keyboards - Film & TV Themes

An exciting collection of hit songs and classic themes from great films and popular TV series.

This entertaining book features Take My Breath Away, La Bamba, Who's That Girl, The Way We Were, Love Theme from 'Superman', Bergerac, Dallas, L.A. Law — plus many more great film and TV themes for you to play and enjoy.

Playing Keyboards - Christmas Songbook

A sparkling collection of favourite Christmas songs and carols for you to enjoy with your family and friends.

Includes: Mary's Boy Child, When A Child Is Born, Silent Night, Good King Wenceslas, Away In A Manger, The Holly And The Ivy, We Three Kings — plus 18 more popular Christmas songs and carols.

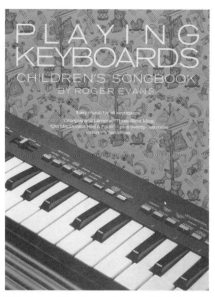

Playing Keyboards - Children's Songbook

A wonderful collection of ever-popular children's songs. Easy to play and fun to sing, you'll soon have everyone singing along with your playing.

Includes: Oranges And Lemons, Three Blind Mice, Old MacDonald Had A Farm, There's A Hole In My Bucket — plus twenty-four more. Complete with full words.

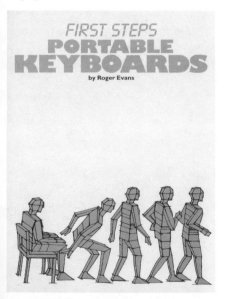

First Steps Portable Keyboards

Roger Evans' pocket size tutor teaches you to play easy music on your keyboard.

No previous musical knowledge is needed. Clear instructions plus helpful hints and friendly advice mean you can start playing straightaway.

The optional cassette makes learning to play even easier, quicker — and even more fun!

How To Read Music - by Roger Evans

This easy to follow book takes the mystery out of music.

It is for absolute beginners — and for those who know something about music and want to learn more. Everything is explained in easy stages so you can quickly learn to read all kinds of music.

How To Read Music includes well-known tunes, and it even shows you how to choose your own music.

How To Play Piano - by Roger Evans

This entertaining book is for everyone who would like to play the piano. It is for absolute beginners — and for those who once started to play and would like to take up the piano again.

How To Play Piano has clear instructions, helpful hints and over 30 well-known tunes to play. It makes learning to play the piano real fun!

Printed by Watkiss Studios Ltd., Biggleswade, Beds. 5/93